Five in the bed

Penny Dann

There were five in the bed,
And the little one said,

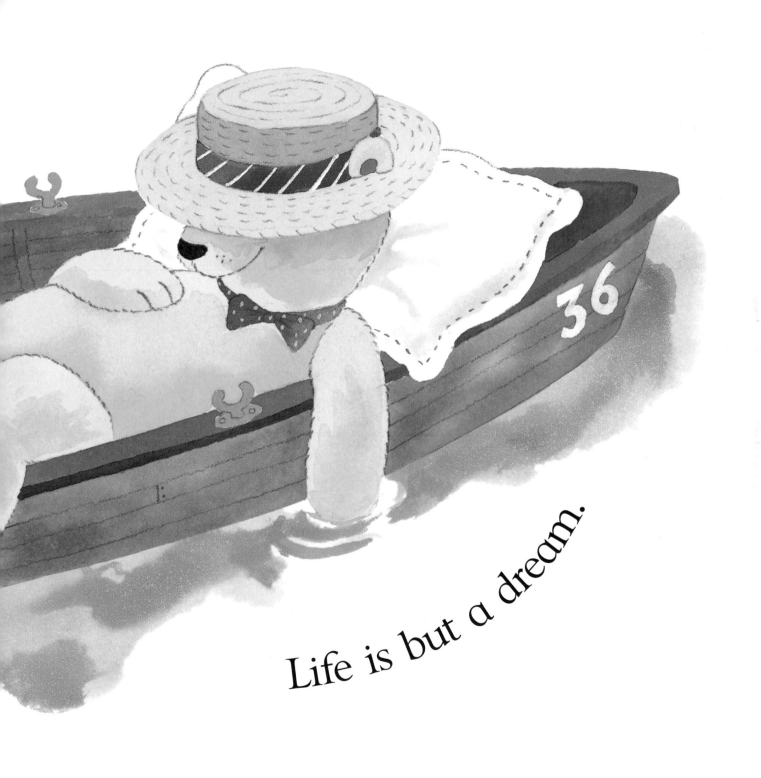

Life is but a dream.

Row, row, row your boat,

Gently out to sea;

BACK

Merrily, merrily, merrily, merrily

Then come back with me.

Row, row, row your boat,

Gently on the tide;

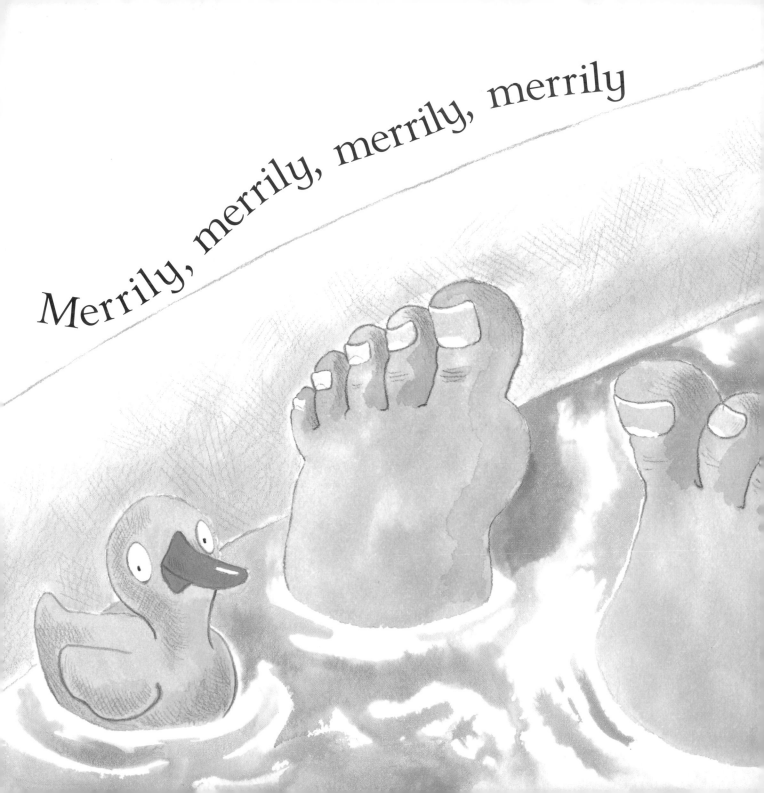

Merrily, merrily, merrily, merrily

To the other side.

Row, row, row your boat,

Gently back to shore;

Merrily, merrily, merrily, merrily

Row, row, row your boat

Penny Dann

Row, row, row your boat,

Gently down the stream;

Merrily, merrily, merrily, merrily

They all rolled over,
And one fell out
Then gave a little shout.

So there were four in the bed,
And the little one said,

They all rolled over,
And one fell out
Then gave a little shout.

So there were three in the bed,
And the little one said,

Roll over, roll over!

They all rolled over,
And one fell out

Then gave a little shout.

So there were two in the bed,
And the little one said,

They all rolled over,
And one fell out
Then gave a little shout.

So there was one in the bed,
Who turned over and said,

Now they've rolled out,
There's room to move about.

So he stretched and smiled...

Then gave a
BIG shout!